HUNGRY HUDSON HAS A CHOICE

Leslie Mitchell Assini

Illustrations by Andy Yura

This book is dedicated to my husband Joe,
my daughters Abigail and Clara, and our dog Piper.
Thank you to my Canadian family for your wonderful
suggestions, support, and encouragement.

A CHARACTER PETS BOOK
A Division of LJM Communications
Hungry Hudson Has a Choice. Copyright © 2021 by Leslie Mitchell Assini.

Book layout & formatting by Aaxel Author Services & VeeVee Creative Studio

ISBN 978-0-578-85094-8

Hudson is a dog with a twinkle in his eye.

If you saw him you would smile, he is just that kind of guy.

He is smart and cuddly and handsome too.

He can have fun with anything, even an old shoe.

1

Hudson's best friend is a boy named Ben.
They play from morning until the day's end.
They run and wrestle and dig holes in the dirt.
They climb and jump and find things they can squirt.

Now, no dog is perfect, we know this is true.
Dogs can be grumpy and naughty too!
Even though Hudson is fun and so sweet,
he makes poor decisions when he wants to eat.

5

At family parties he can be quite the pest,
munching on snacks, leaving none for the guests.
There was the time he ate the whole holiday ham,
and the fried eggs and bacon while still in the pan!
He can eat big pots of chili, entire blueberry pies,
and gobble them up in the blink of an eye.

6

7

But there was one time, not so long ago,
Hudson saw a cake topped with candles all aglow.
It was a birthday cake for his very best friend,
the one, the only, the wonderful Ben.

9

What happened next was really the worst.
Hudson pounced on the cake and made it burst!
Chunks of cake flew everywhere.
Onto the walls, the ceiling, and in everyone's hair.

11

"Oh Hudson," said Ben. "Look what you've done!
You're supposed to be my friend, but you've ruined all the fun."
Hudson saw the sad look in his best friend's eyes.
With the cake now a mess, Ben started to cry.

Hudson felt so terrible, he wanted to hide in the mud.
How could I do that? he thought. *Ben's my best bud!*
What happened that day made Hudson ashamed.
He knew he had no one but himself to blame.

13

From that point on, when it came to food,
Hudson tried his best not to be so rude.

But could a dog learn new tricks? Or was it too late?
Hudson was put to the test on an important date.
For soon there would be another birthday for Ben.
With a great big cake... but would Hudson make trouble again?

When the day of the party finally arrived,
the house was busy like a honeybee hive.
From inside the kitchen came the cake's sweet scent.
Hudson followed his nose, and towards the cake he went.

17

First, he smelled the sugar, then he smelled the cream.
Hudson thought the cake was like something from a dream.
The cake was chocolate with marshmallow topping,
and covered in candy and caramel frosting.
Hudson stared at the cake and started to drool.
If Hudson ate that cake would he be breaking a rule?

18

19

Hudson looked to his left, he looked to his right.
There was no one around, there was no one in sight.
Hudson sat all alone, with the cake looking yummy.
He couldn't stop thinking about that cake in his tummy.

He said to himself, *All I want is a little lick!*
Or I could start with a bite and then eat it up quick!
No one will notice, it's not a big deal.
Who says you need cake after a birthday meal?

Hudson stepped up to the cake with his mouth opened wide.

He was about to take a bite when he heard Ben laughing outside.

Hudson looked out the window and saw Ben having fun.

It made him think about what good friends they'd become.

He thought, *If I eat this cake it will make everyone mad,*

and worst of all, my friend Ben will be sad.

Again, I'm only thinking of me,

and really, what kind of friend would I be?

Hudson took a deep breath and gave himself a shake.

He put his paws on the floor and stepped away from that cake.

Then in through the door walked the birthday boy.
Ben saw the cake and Hudson, and his face filled with joy.
He started laughing as the whole party ran in.
"Happy Birthday!" they sang with big smiles and grins.

25

"I'm so proud of you, Hudson!" Ben said with glee.
"You could have eaten my cake, but instead you thought of me."
Ben gave Hudson a hug and some tasty treats.
Then they sat down together and that cake they did eat!

As Hudson sat happily licking his dish,
he was glad he had chosen not to be so selfish.
Hudson loved Ben, and Ben loved him too.
And on that day Hudson learned to think of others,
because that's what friends do.

About the Author

Leslie Mitchell Assini is a writer and communications professional in Denver, Colorado. She lives with her husband, two daughters, a dog, 10 fish and a lizard. Hungry Hudson is inspired by real-life dogs, real-life messes, and how we can learn and grow together. This is Leslie's first children's book.
Connect with Leslie on Facebook: @lesmitchellassini

About the Illustrator

Andy Yura is an illustrator living in Malang, Indonesia. He is currently studying visual communication design focusing on children's book illustration. At the moment Andy does not have any pets, but he plans to have a cat when he finishes his studies!
Connect with Andy on Instagram: @andyura_

Manufactured by Amazon.ca
Bolton, ON

19823717R00021